Pepe the Key West Rooster

Written by Victoria Scudder
Illustrated by Nita Candra

Scout & Company Publishing

"One Human Family"... and roosters, too!

ISBN: 979-8-9862023-9-6

For additional publications from Scout & Company, visit:

The sun rose in the east,
across the blue sea.
"A cockle doodle doo,"
says little 'ol me.

My name is Pepe,
a rooster, I'll tell.
Born in Key West,
a wee cockerel.

My home is an island,
a place I roam free.
My life is so sweet
by the gumbo limbo tree.

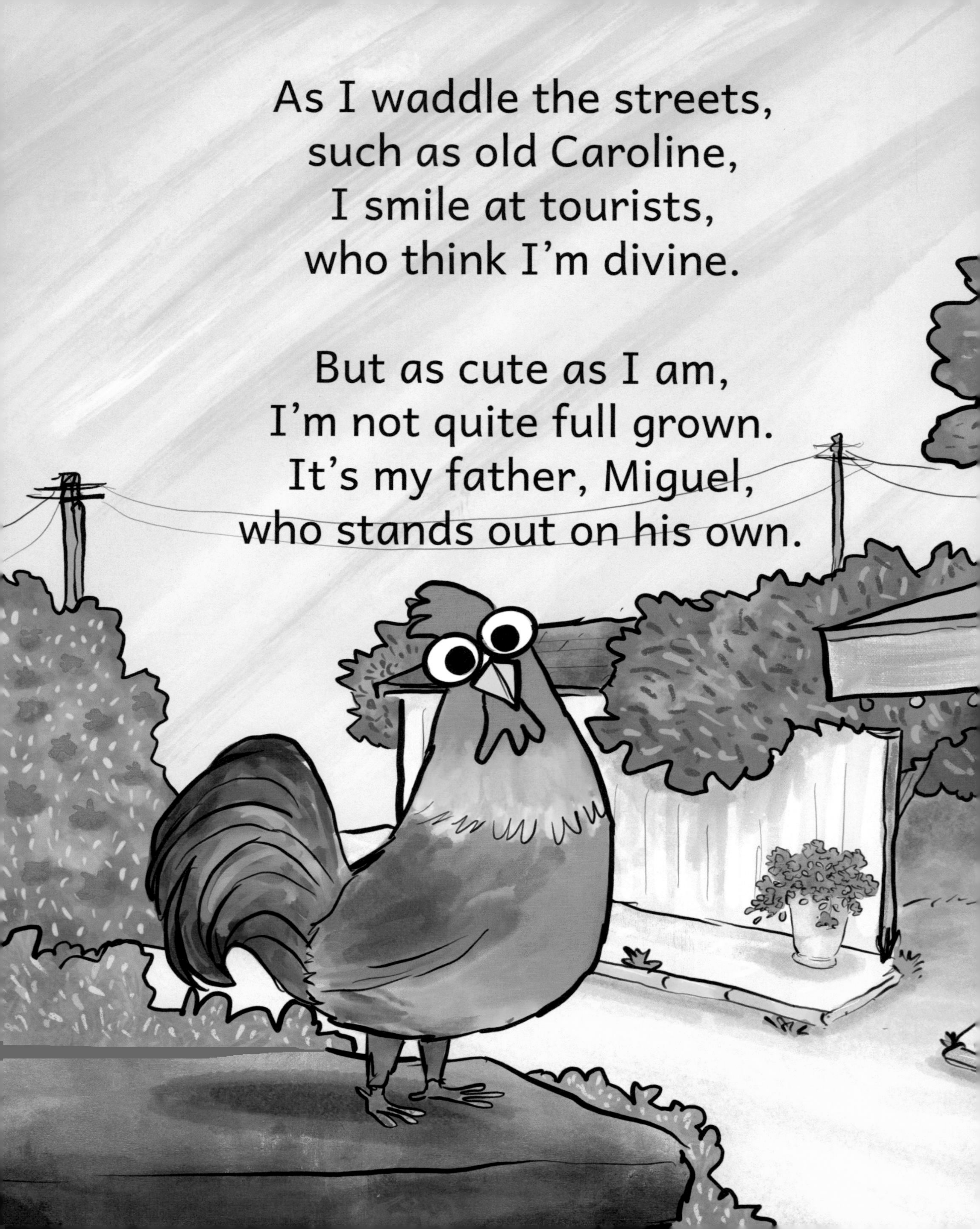

As I waddle the streets,
such as old Caroline,
I smile at tourists,
who think I'm divine.

But as cute as I am,
I'm not quite full grown.
It's my father, Miguel,
who stands out on his own.

EAT
PEPE'S
Meals

Miguel is the one
our visitors like to see.
He has a red comb
much bigger than me.

His feathers are colored,
while mine are plain brown.
And he'll puff them up big
while we're strolling 'bout town.

I admire my father.
As his son, I'm so proud.
But how can little me
stand out in this crowd?

So I start on a trek,
'round my beautiful isle,
to search for an answer
within a square mile.

At the Southernmost Point,
by the famous red buoy,
I pause for a moment
then see my friend Huey.

"Pepe," calls the parrot,
"I'm so happy to see you!
Let's climb up the lighthouse
and check out the view!"

"That sounds fun, mi *amigo*!
But let's do that next time.
And let's start with some pie -
Kermit's yummy key lime!"

I'm off on a mission
and in quite a hurry.
There's a trolley to catch,
and I'd like to be early.

MILE
0
"All aboard, hop aboard!"
Trolley Tim hollers out.
"Adventures await
when you're on the right
route!"

To Hemingway's house,
an author of prose,
where I find my friend, Kitty,
and her famous six toes.

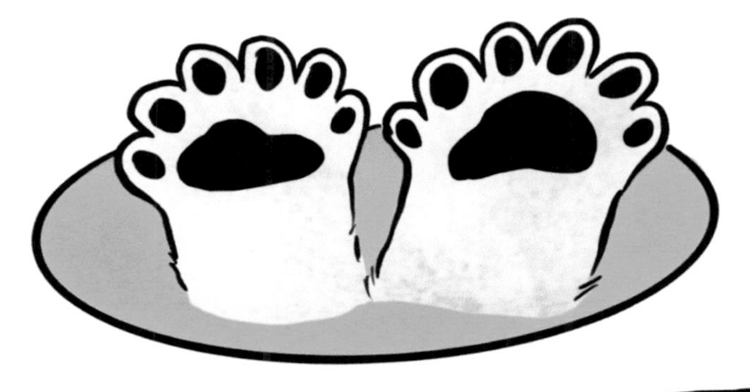

I ask the old cat
what it's like to be cool,
but she tells me I'm silly
then curls up on her stool.

With no help from that cat,
I ride next to the pier.
My pelican friends
might make it more clear.

“How can I be special?”
I ask my friend, Skip.
“Perhaps I could dive
to Mel’s treasure ship?”

"The Atocha, you mean?
The one full of gold?
An air tank you'll need,
but that's really quite bold."

"Sweet little rooster,"
caws Skip's friend, Monroe.
"You don't need doubloons
or to put on a show."

I think about that and
decide a dive's not for me.
So I ride over next
to the great banyan tree.

"Little bird, hummingbird,
what can I try?
I want to be special.
Will you teach me to fly?"

"Pepe, you have wings;
they might be small yet.
But as you get older,
it's nothing to sweat."

I'm not sure I like this
waiting long to grow up.
So off to Mallory Square,
to shake off my slump.

At sunset there are jugglers,
magicians, and clowns.
I can get my face painted
or hear musicians from town.

As I look at the ocean,
I start smiling inside.
The day's almost over,
but I feel full of pride.

I love Cayo Hueso!
It's paradise, you see.
And I had a fun day
learning more about me.

I might still be little,
but I see that's okay.
For as a wee cockerel,
I have more time to play!

A Bit of Key West Trivia

The Roosters

The rooster, which symbolizes good luck, wealth, good fortune, and hope, is the unofficial mascot for Key West. Roosters were brought to the island from Cuba in the 1860s for sport and eventually released into the wild to strut their colorful stuff. Since then, they've become some of the island's most favorite and funkiest of feathered friends. They are legally protected to spread their good vibes everywhere they go.

The Gumbo Limbo Tree

Gumbo limbo trees are nature's cool kids, offering shade and cozy homes to all sorts of animals. Did you know they can live to be 100 years old? With their mighty roots, they stand tall even in the wildest storms (and several hurricanes!). They're the real superheroes of Key West's ecosystem, protecting and nurturing life in their leafy embrace.

Caroline Street

Caroline Street has been around since way back in the 1800s and was named after one of the super adventurous Whitehead siblings. Caroline's big bro John Whitehead got shipwrecked off of the island in 1819 and later decided, "Hey, let's make a street!" So now we have this awesome road with a history as exciting as a pirate's treasure map.

Pepe's Cafe

Pepe's Cafe, established in 1909, is the oldest eatery in the Florida Keys and second oldest in the State of Florida! It has survived the Great Depression and both World Wars on Duval Street before it was moved to its current location on Caroline Street in the 1950s.
Note: The restaurant has no relation to Pepe the rooster.

The Southernmost Point of the Continental USA

The famous black, yellow, and red striped buoy marker marks the tippy, tippy southernmost point of the continental United States! It's located roughly 90 miles north of Havana, Cuba, making it closer to our Cuban neighbors than to Miami, Florida. Some people say they can see Cuba from the marker, but not really. The curve of the earth makes it fall below the horizon. If you're lucky, however, you just might see the faint glow of Havana's city lights!

Key West Lighthouse

The Key West lighthouse is like a tall, stripey ice cream cone standing guard over the island. It has a unique story too - did you know that it was actually moved from its original location closer to the coast? Yep, the town wanted to keep it safe from the sneaky waves, so they moved it inland where it stands tall and proud today.

Kermit's Key Lime Shoppe

This longtime Key West staple is filled with the aroma of tangy key limes and loyal customers trying to unravel the secret to their mouthwatering recipes. It's been recognized as having the best Key Lime Pie by Food Network, National Geographic, and Paula Deen!

Hemingway's House and the 6-Toed Cats

Back in the 1930s, a ship's captain gifted the legendary author Ernest Hemingway a special white cat with six toes. That cat, named Snow White, began a six-toed legacy still living in the Hemingway House today. If you ever visit, make sure to look for Snow White's great-great-great grand kitties!

The Atocha Treasure Ship

The Nuestra Senora de Atocha was a Spanish treasure ship that sank in a storm off the coast of Key West. It carried a crazy big fortune in gold doubloons and precious gems. In 1971, super cool treasure hunter, Mel Fisher, started searching for the shipwreck. He and his team finally found it in 1985, and the value of its treasures is estimated at about $400 million. That's a lot of doubloons!

The Banyan Tree

The Banyan tree is the ultimate master of expansion! It's not your ordinary tree. Instead of starting from a tiny seed, it takes a different approach. It acts like a sneaky vine and uses "host" plants to weave its roots and branches together. It's like the tree is taking a stroll, finding new spots to settle down and grow. The largest in the world is located in its native India, covers an area about as big as a baseball field, and is 250 years old!

Mallory Square Sunset Celebration

At Mallory Square, get ready for an awesome sunset show! All evening long, 7 days a week, you'll find talented performers, island crafts, and even pirates! Grrr! The sky turns into a bright painting with amazing colors. As the sun says goodbye and disappears into the ocean, the crowd bursts into cheers and applause, celebrating the end of another beautiful day in paradise.

Cayo Hueso

Cayo Hueso is the Spanish term for Key West, though once upon a time it also meant “bone island.” Spooky, right? While Key West does have its fair share of ghostly stories, Cayo Hueso sounded so much like “Key West” to English ears that the name eventually stuck.

About the Author

I didn't plan on becoming a book author for young children. Honestly.

I retired from the Air Force after 20 years of service, spent 15 years as a classroom teacher, and now run my own company that has nothing to do with either, but I do love to write! Always have.

Stories come to me in rushes now and, at any given moment, I have multiple projects in the works at once. I'm even working on my first middle-grade historical fiction series! If you want to hop on this crazy bandwagon and follow along, sign up for my newsletter at www.Victoria-Scudder.com. I promise not to bombard you, and I'll always make it fun!

I hope you enjoyed reading about Pepe's journey as much as I had fun writing about it.

For additional updates, visit www.facebook.com/scoutandcompanypublishing/.

Author website: www.Victoria-Scudder.com

Do you have a fun pic of you or your kiddo with Pepe? Send me a copy at scoutandcompanyflorida@gmail.com, and I'll post it on my socials!

Additional Titles

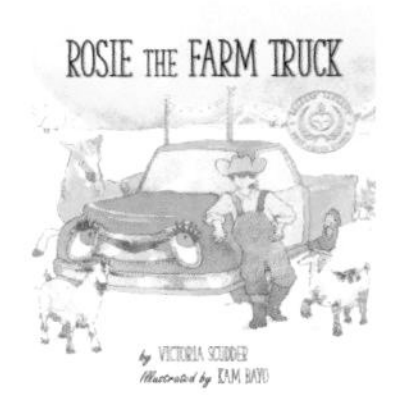

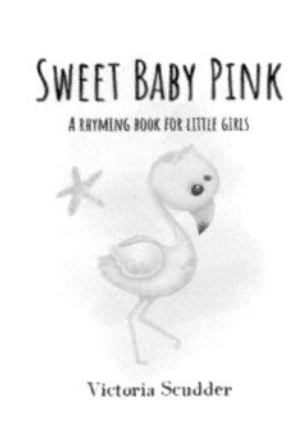

Resources

For study guides and additional resources, as well as special bonuses, please visit:
www.facebook.com/scoutandcompanypublishing/
and
www.Victoria-Scudder.com

Your reviews mean a LOT to me as an Indie author! Please take a moment to log into Amazon and review my book. This helps Pepe get seen! Make a rooster happy - spread the word!

Review this product

Share your thoughts with other customers

Write a customer review

Made in the USA
Columbia, SC
05 February 2024